LUCY DANIELS

ANIMAL ARK™
CLASSICS

PUPPY IN A PUDDLE

Hodder Children's Books

a division of Hachette Children's Books

The format details for this book are;
Comic Sans, Normal 36, Single Spacing

To my best friend Tristan Chapman and Hugo, his wonderful big puppy.

Special thanks to Ingrid Hoare
Thanks also to C. J. Hall, B. Vet.Med., M.R.C.VS., for reviewing the veterinary information contained in this book.

First published in Great Britain in 1999
by Hodder Children's Books
This edition published in 2006

A Catalogue record for this book is available from the British Library

ISBN-10: 0340 88160 7
ISBN-13: 978 0 340 88160 6

Typeset in Baskerville by Avon DataSet Ltd.
Bidford-on-Avon, Warwickshire

Hodder Children's Books
a division of Hachette Children's Books
338 Euston Road

London NW1 3BH

The Charity is unique in its focus on young people who face different challenges as they grow up. The Guide Dogs for the Blind Association is special in that it offers solutions, tailored to individual needs.

Technological developments create possible new learning experiences for the visually impaired, but too often these life - changing aids are beyond the financial reach of many families. The Guide Dogs for the Blind Association provides a vital service, ensuring through the supply of specially adapted computers, large print books, advice and grants that children receive the help they really need.

If you would like to help The Guide Dogs for the Blind Association in any way at all, please contact our offices on 0800 688 8405. We look forward to your call.

The Guide Dogs for the Blind Association would like to acknowledge their appreciation to the publisher, the author and the illustrator for donating the digital files to allow the reproduction of this book for children and young adults with visual difficulties.

A Note from Lucy Daniels

Dear readers,

I'm so excited that Hodder Children's Books is publishing your favourite titles as Animal Ark Classics. I can't believe it's ten years since Mandy and James had their first adventure. I've written so many stories about them they feel like real friends to me now and it's been such fun thinking up new stories for them both.

I know from your letters how much you enjoy sharing their love of animals. As you can tell, I'm a huge fan of animals myself, and can't imagine a day when I will ever want to stop writing about them.

Happy reading!

Very best wishes,

Lucy

Contents

Four

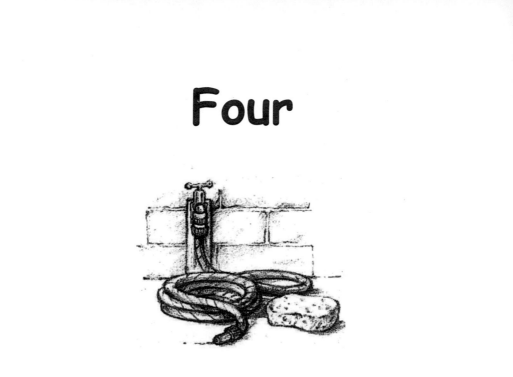

The days
leading up to the
end of term were
very busy and

seemed to go by in a blur as Mandy and James planned for the dog wash. They decided to spread the word about the fund-raising event as far and

wide as possible.
They put up
posters in the
waiting-room at
Animal Ark, on
the school notice-
board, in
Welford's post

office and in the church porch.

When John Hardy had arrived home from school, Mandy and James called round to see him at the

Fox and Goose.
He was as excited
about the dog
wash as they
were.

'Dad's going to
move things about
a bit in here on
the day,' he told

Mandy and James, leading them outside to the large walled garden. 'He's making space for us to wash the dogs near the tap here. We're going to put out extra chairs for the dog owners and there will be umbrellas for shade if it's hot.'

'Let's hope so,' said James.

'We're going to get pretty wet.'

'It doesn't matter,' Mandy told them. 'It's going to be great fun. Let's just hope lots of people turn up.'

'I saw your poster, James,' John said. 'It looks really good.' James's face flushed pink with embarrassment.

'Thanks,' he mumbled.

'Everything's going to plan,' Mandy said happily. 'All we have to hope for now is that it doesn't pour with rain on Saturday!'

The Saturday of the dog wash dawned bright and sunny. When Mandy looked out of the bedroom window, there wasn't a cloud in the sky and she heaved a sigh of relief. A rainy day would have spoilt .everything.

Mandy was just clearing away the breakfast dishes when there was a knock at the kitchen door. Mrs Hope answered the door to James, and Blackie bounded into the kitchen. The Labrador seized one of Adam Hope's

tennis shoes and
paraded about
with it in his
mouth.

'He's really
excited,' James
apologised,
puffing, as he

grabbed at the shoe.

'He's excited!' Emily Hope laughed, glancing at Mandy. 'Then it must be infectious.'

James was wearing a pair of shorts and a T-shirt. He held up a plastic carrier bag to show Mandy. 'I brought a change of clothes - in case we get soaked,' he told her.

'Good idea!' she laughed. 'Well, we'd better go. We've got to be ready to start by eleven, and it's

ten o'clock now.
We'll need time
to set things up.'
    'I'm ready,'
James told her.
'Jenny arrived
last night. She's
going to meet us
there.'

Mandy picked up
a carrier bag
filled with plastic
bottles of dog
shampoo. 'Will
you make sure
Dad comes over in
time for the

start, Mum?' she asked.

Emily Hope nodded. 'He's got a few things to do in the surgery - but he'll be there. I hope it all goes smoothly. I'll come over as soon as surgery is finished,' she promised. 'Have fun!'

'We will. Thanks,' called Mandy, as the kitchen door

slammed loudly behind her.

The garden of the Fox and Goose had been transformed. Mr Hardy had moved the wooden tables, benches and assorted chairs to the far end, leaving plenty of room for a crowd of excited dogs and their owners.

Mandy beamed, looking around at the garden. 'Oh,

this is brilliant. Thank you!'

'Well, it's for a good cause,' Sara Hardy smiled, surveying the pile of equipment that James had just dumped on the grass.

'Sara,' John asked, 'can we use that big table in the kitchen to put out here? Don't you think we'll need a table, Mandy?'

'Yes. Someone will have to stand behind it and take the money as people come in,' Mandy agreed. 'Maybe Dad can do that. James has got a big glass jar from his mum to put the money in.'

'Right,' John said, in his best businesslike manner. 'I'll go

and get the table.
Will you help me,
James?'

'OK,' said
James. 'Can I
leave Blackie
loose out here,
Mrs Hardy?'

'Yes, he'll be
fine in the garden.
He can't get out.'
Sara Hardy
smiled.

'Here's Jenny!'
Mandy called,
rushing over to
meet James's

cousin at the gate. They had met when Mandy had gone with James to spend a week's holiday in the Welsh fishing village where Jenny lived.

'Hello, Mandy,' Jenny said, a bit shyly, in her soft Welsh accent. She wore her dark hair in bunches, just as Mandy remembered her.

'Hi, Jenny!'
Mandy smiled.
'Thanks for
coming. It's great
to see you. I'm
really glad we've
got you to help.
Would you mind
hanging this sign

on the gate for me? It's nearly eleven time for people to start arriving.'

'Important! Please keep gate closed,' Jenny read. 'OK.' She

grinned and
hurried off to
the gate.

'Mandy!' James
said urgently.
'Look! There are
people here
already.' Mandy
looked. A couple

she didn't know
had come
hesitantly
through the gate
and into the
garden. They had
a big, hairy
mongrel on a lead.

'Are you open yet?' the woman inquired. 'Only, we were passing and saw your poster...'

'Certainly!' grinned Mandy. 'Bring him in. It's

three pounds for each dog. What's his name?'

'Mucky,' said the woman, ruffling the dog's coat affectionately. 'And it suits him!

He's in need of a good wash, I'm afraid.'

James had taken off his shoes in preparation for a good soaking. 'How does Mucky feel about being washed?' he asked cautiously, taking the mongrel's lead.

'Oh, he loves a bath; don't you, Mucky?' grinned the man.

Mandy was relieved. At least their first customer wouldn't be a tricky one. She spotted her father chatting to Julian Hardy

and waved to him.
'Dad! We've got
out first
customer!'
    'Great!' said Mr
Hope, smiling.
'Well, get to it,
and send them
over my way to

pay when you're finished, will you?'

In no time at all, the garden was filled with chatting people and excited dogs. Mandy could

hardly believe
how many people
had seen their
posters.
Welford's dog
owners had
turned out in
force to support
them, and there

were quite a few strangers among the crowd too.

Mr Markham, the chairman of the parish council, brought his beagle Bunty to be washed, and there was a difficult moment when the beagle tried to frighten Miss Martin's Yorkshire terrier, Snap. Betty Hilder brought a young rescued mongrel from her animal sanctuary, and even Mrs Ponsonby came, with Pandora tucked under her arm and Toby straining on a lead.

Mandy, James, Jenny and John got to work and they soon had an efficient production line going. Pet owners were strolling about with cold drinks in their hands, as they waited for their dogs' turn.

'Sara says my dad's going to give a donation to the fund because of the extra money he made in the pub,' John reported, as he joined Mandy who was rinsing off a corgi called Jack.

'Oh, that's great!' Mandy said gratefully.

The dog wash was going to be a huge success.

'Look who's next,' hissed James, above the sound of yapping. Mandy glanced up to see Ernie Bell holding Pandora the Pekinese. Mrs Ponsonby hovered nearby, looking worried. She wore a wide brimmed straw hat decorated with silk flowers.

'I don't believe it,' Mandy gasped. 'Mrs Ponsonby is going to let us wash Pandora,' she whispered.

'Really, Mr Bell...' Mrs Ponsonby was

protesting. 'I don't think Pandora will appreciate the hose one bit. She prefers a bath of warm...'

'Now, Mrs Ponsonby,'

soothed Ernie, interrupting her. He stroked Pandora's head and she panted all the harder. 'I reckon she'll love a cool shower on a hot day like this.

You just leave her to me. We'll soon have her looking as elegant as you are. And may I say that's a very handsome hat you're wearing today, Mrs P?'

'Oh, thank you,' trilled Mrs Ponsonby, smiling broadly. Then her smile faded and she looked very severe. 'Now, you will take care

with my Pandora,
won't you?'

Mandy laughed
and whispered to
the others,
'Ernie's been
flattering Mrs
Ponsonby. That's
how he's

persuaded her to let us wash Pandora!' She let go of the corgi's collar and the little dog tore off to find a patch of green grass to roll on.

'You're doing a great job.' Mandy heard Emily Hope's voice and looked up to see

her mother
smiling down at
them.

'Oh, Mum!' said
Mandy. 'You got
here. It seems to
be going really
well.'

'Let me give you a tip.' Mrs Hope spoke softly. 'Use just a sponge on Pandora. You don't want to get shampoo in her eyes.'

'No, we don't,' James said, grimacing.

Mandy could just imagine the scene with Mrs Ponsonby if anything happened to Pandora.

The Pekinese submitted meekly to the wet sponge, while Ernie Bell offered advice from a nearby bench. 'Wet her properly!' he urged Mandy. 'Give her a proper bath. She's a dog, not a doll!'

'Ernest Bell!' scolded Mrs Ponsonby, trying to keep Toby

from joining in
Pandora's bath.

'Pandora
doesn't like water,
I tell you. Don't
interfere!'

Two hours later,
Mandy had lost

count of the number of dogs they had washed. She was hot and tired but she was enjoying herself so much she didn't care. As she looked around the garden, she noticed that there were only a few dogs still waiting for their turn.

'Phew!' gasped James, sitting back on the grass.

'It feels like we've washed every dog in Yorkshire!'

'I think we might have,' said John, passing round the tray of cold drinks that

Sara had given him. Mandy took one of the plastic cups and drank gratefully.

'My fingers are numb,' Jenny announced.

'Hmm, mine too,' Mandy said, examining them as she crunched on a piece of ice.

'Just one more to go, everyone,' said Mr Hardy. 'I think that's the lot, after this next little fellow. Every dog in Welford must be squeaky-clean - well done!'

The last dog to be washed was a small, nervous

cocker spaniel. He shook his head vigorously, sending suds of shampoo flying off his long, curly - haired ears. Mandy and James rinsed him off as quickly as possible and gave him back to his Owner, who was hovering nearby, holding a towel she had brought with her.

At last, it was over. Mandy sat

down in the wet and soapy grass, exhausted. 'That was fun,' she said, grinning at her friends. 'But I'm glad we're finished.'

'Me too,' James sighed. 'I'm soaked through.'

'At least it's a hot day,' Jenny said. 'I wouldn't have fancied getting this wet otherwise.'

'What a team!' John said, patting James on the back. 'We could go into business.'

'NO thank you,' James said firmly. 'I feel as if I'll never get rid of

the smell of dog
shampoo!'

Mandy stood up
slowly and
stretched. She
went to take the
notice off the
gate. Water from
the hose had run

down the gently sloping lawn and collected at the wooden gate. The tap had been turned off but it was still trickling under the bottom of the gate and into the car park beyond.

'Oops,' Mandy muttered to herself. 'I think we've probably flooded Mr Hardy's carpark.' She unlatched the gate and peered out. The water had streamed out and formed an impressive puddle on the uneven surface of the tarred forecourt.

As Mandy looked around, she gasped.

A puppy was sitting in a shallow puddle just to the right of her bare feet. Mandy looked down at its miserable little face, and the tangled, shaggy coat. She gathered the little dog gently into her arms. Its feet splayed out with fear as Mandy picked it up. Then, feeling the warmth of her arms, it began to relax against her. The puppy snuggled closer, shivering, and

gave a tiny
whimper.

'Oh!' Mandy
said softly. 'Oh,
you poor little
thing. What are
you doing here?
You're only a few
weeks old! Where

have you come from?'

The pup looked a little bit like Rush, but Mandy could feel the bones through this pup's skin and she remembered the plump, cuddly feel of the well-fed little Rush. This puppy had been neglected. Its fur was matted and its belly was swollen beneath the skinny rib cage - a sign of worms, Mandy remembered.

Mandy felt a hot flush of anger surge through her. 'Who,' she asked the little dog, 'would let you get into this state?' She glared around, peering into the few remaining parked cars, searching for the puppy's owner.

There was no one about.

Moving very gently, Mandy carried the little puppy through the gate into the garden. 'James!'

she called. 'Come quickly!'

Five

James and the others were clearing up. Mandy saw him

wheel round when he heard the urgency in her voice. He hurried over to where she was standing just inside the gate, cradling the shivering puppy protectively.

'What on earth have you got there?' James called, as he came towards her.

'It's an Old English sheepdog

puppy,' Mandy said. 'I found it sitting in a puddle outside the gate.'

'All alone? In the carpark?' James asked. 'Any sign of the owner?' He put out a finger and stroked the pup's head lightly. The puppy shrank back and buried its nose in Mandy's forearm.

'No, everyone's gone. Let's go and

find my mum and dad,' Mandy said.

'They're over there, in the garden with Mr Hardy,' James told her.

Adam Hope looked up and

called out to Mandy as she approached. 'You've done really well - you've collected £105!' he told her.

'Never mind about that, Dad,' Mandy cried. 'Look what I've found!'

Mrs Hope, Sara and Julian Hardy, and John and Jenny, who had been collecting up glasses from the garden, gathered around her. The puppy, alarmed at all the strange faces, squirmed uncomfortably, then edged its way upward and snuggled under Mandy's chin.

'A lost puppy?' Emily Hope frowned in concern. 'Looks in a bit of a mess, doesn't it?'

'Lost - or abandoned,' Mandy said unhappily. 'There's no one around who could own it and it doesn't have a name tag. And

look at it, Mum,
it's in a terrible
state!'

Blackie raised
his nose and tried
to sniff at the
interesting bundle,
as Emily Hope
lifted the puppy

gently from
Mandy's arms.
'About twelve or
thirteen weeks
old, I would
guess,' said
Mandy's mum.
She ran her
fingers lightly

around the
puppy's frail body
and looked at the
rims of its blue
eyes. 'Poor thing!
I guess you've
been wandering
about for a while
- you're very

thin.' Mrs Hope paused and lifted the puppy to peer at its rather swollen tummy. 'It's a girl,' she told them.

'Oh, it's so sweet,' Jenny said.

'Shall I go and have a look around outside - see if I can spot anyone who might know something about it?' John asked.

'I've looked,' said Mandy, 'and I'm sure there's no one about.'

Adam Hope took the puppy from his wife, checking its coat for signs of fleas. Mandy stood beside him and James, while Jenny and John hovered nearby, looking worried.

'She might be in need of some liquid if she's a stray. I think

we'd better get
her to the
surgery and have
a proper look at
her,' Mr Hope
said at last.

'Can I come
with you?' James
asked.

'I'll go with John,' Jenny said. 'We'll see if we can find anyone in the village who knows where she came from.'

'I've got just the name for

you,' said Mandy, peering at the little pup. 'We'll call, you Puddles.'

Mrs Hope raised her eyebrows. 'Mandy, you know the rules...'

Mandy knew she was not supposed to give stray animals names, but she was determined that the defenceless, abandoned puppy should be cared for now. 'She should have a name - that's the least she deserves,' she protested.

'You go on back to Animal Ark,' Sara Hardy said,

putting a hand on Mandy's shoulder. 'Julian and I will finish clearing up here. And if anyone comes looking for a puppy, we'll send them straight over to you.'

Back at the surgery, the puppy seemed more nervous than ever. She wiggled about in

Mandy's arms, trying to hide by burying her head. Mandy spoke soothingly to her, and Puddles responded gratefully by licking Mandy's chin.

Adam Hope examined her carefully. 'She needs a good wash, Mandy,' he said. 'She's had tummy trouble

and she's rather
dehydrated and
weak. I'll give her
a worming
medicine and put
her on a drip to
get some fluid
into her.'

'Can't I feed her, Dad?' Mandy pleaded. 'She's so thin — she must be starving.'

'Not just yet, love. We'll try her on a small amount of food a bit later. Let's see how she responds to the fluid first.'

Mandy stood with James, watching the puppy hunched miserably on the examination table. Puddles hung her head, refusing to look at them. 'How can people be so cruel?' James asked, angrily.

'It never ceases to amaze me, James,' Mr Hope sighed, 'but they can - and they are.'

'This is the second Old English sheepdog

puppy in some
kind of trouble,'
Mandy said.

'You're right,
Mandy,'
confirmed Mrs
Hope, glancing at
her husband.
'This puppy would

be about the same age as the deaf puppy that came in to see you - Rush, was it?'

'That's right,' said Adam Hope, peering into Puddles' ear. 'Mr

Taylor brought Rush in about let's see... three weeks ago now. It might be a coincidence, but this pup could easily have been a littermate to

little Rush.
Luckily, this
puppy has
perfectly good
hearing.'
   'It's that Mrs
Merrick again!'
Mandy declared

furiously. 'That woman...'

'Hold on, Mandy.' Mrs Hope held up her hand. 'We have no idea whether this poor scrap has anything to do with Mrs Merrick. You can't go around blaming people when we don't have the facts.'

'Well,' Mandy began, 'she breeds Old

English sheepdogs, doesn't she?'

'That's no evidence at all,' Adam Hope pointed out gently. 'This puppy may have been abandoned from a car by her owners as they passed through Welford. Or she may have escaped from home. Someone might be going frantic looking for her.'

'It's strange that she turned up at the Fox and Goose just as we were having the dog wash,' James mused.

'Mum, do you think somebody

put her out of a car at the pub because they knew there would be dog lovers there?' Mandy asked.

Emily Hope put an arm round

Mandy. 'I don't know, love. The main thing is, she's safe with us here now. We'll take care of her.'

There was a soft knocking on the door of the

treatment room and Mandy's heart leaped. Was this Puddles' owner come looking for her?

'Only me. . .' Ted Forrester

put his head
round the door.

'Hello, Ted!'
said Mr and Mrs
Hope together. 'I
stopped in at the
Fox and Goose
and Mrs Hardy
told me about the

puppy Mandy found,' Ted told them. 'Anything I can do?'

'We were just discussing how it might have got there, Ted,' Adam Hope said.

'And speculating on whether it might be one of Mrs Merrick's pups. . .' Emily Hope added.

Ted walked over to the

examination table and stooped to look at Puddles. 'Hello there, little un. . .' he began, tipping the little dog's chin up with his finger.

'If it is one of Mrs Merrick's litter,' said Mandy heatedly, as Ted crooned and stroked Puddles, 'then she should be ashamed of

herself! First
breeding a deaf
puppy and now. .'
 'Now, Mandy,'
Ted said,
straightening up
and looking at her.
'I know she
breeds this type

of dog, but we don't know it's one of hers, do we?'

'I suppose not. . .' Mandy mumbled. She knew she was being

unreasonable but she couldn't help herself. She felt sure that Puddles was something to do with the Merrick kennels.

'Mrs Merrick might have sold

this puppy in good faith to someone who decided simply to get rid of it, you know,' Ted continued. 'Have you spoken to Mrs Merrick about

Rush, Ted?' Mr Hope asked.

'I can't say that I have,' admitted Ted. 'It's been a hectic time for me lately - but I will, I promise.'

He glanced at Mandy. 'But we can't go upsetting the lady, mind, by going around making wild accusations.'

'It's a bit of a strange

coincidence,'
Mandy insisted.

'Well, never mind about that. Let's get on with sorting out this puppy, shall we?' Emily Hope said briskly, changing the subject. She steered Mandy towards the basin. 'You run some warm water in there, and I'll get some shampoo. We'll clean her up before we do anything else. OK?'

'How's her health?' Ted asked Adam.

'She's had diarrhoea, so she's very dehydrated. I

would guess she's been wandering for quite a few days. Being so young, she's lucky to be alive,' Adam replied.

'Well, I'll let my colleagues

know. They'll put the word out and maybe an owner will, come forward. And I'll also notify the police, shall I? Anyone who's lost a pet is likely to report it to them.' Ted smiled and turned to Mandy and James.

'Thanks, Ted,' Adam Hope said. 'I suppose I'd better be getting back to the Fox

and Goose. I've
left the money we
collected with
Julian Hardy.'

'I'll let you get
on, then.' Ted
waved from the
door. 'Good luck

with the pup. Bye, all.'

Mandy had half filled the big stainless steel basin with warm water. Puddles' tiny feet scrabbled frantically as she was lowered into it. Mandy felt sorry for the frightened puppy. 'It has to be done,' Mrs Hope said firmly. 'She'll be a lot happier when we've cleaned up the mess she's made of herself.'

'James? Mandy?' Jenny was calling from the waiting-room. 'Are you here?'

'I'll go,' said
James.

'Bring her in
here, if you like,'
Mrs Hope said.
James was back a
moment later,
with Jenny and
John. They

gathered around
the basin, looking
at the bedraggled
little puppy.

'Did you find
anyone who knows
Puddles?' James
asked eagerly.

'Nobody,' Jenny said. 'We asked around - we even knocked on a few doors - but nobody knows anything about her.'

'Most people we asked said to come here - to Animal Ark - for help,' John said.

Mrs Hope washed Puddles as gently as she could. The water

turned a murky grey-brown from the dirt in the puppy's coat. With a wad of cotton wool, Mandy wiped away the encrusted muck round

Puddles' blue eyes. She gazed up at Mandy trustingly.

'What are you going to do?' Jenny asked.

'The RSPCA knows about her,

and they'll let the police know,' Mandy said. 'We'll keep her here with us until she's stronger.'

'Let's hope someone will claim her soon,' Emily

Hope said with a smile, reaching into a cupboard nearby for a towel.

On the treatment table, Mandy patted and gently rubbed

Puddles until the towel had soaked up almost all the water from her coat.

'She looks like a different dog!' John exclaimed. It was true. The puppy's dirty, matted fur was now a snowy white. Mrs Hope began to tease out some of the twisted knots of hair, using her fingers to prise them apart.

'She's so tired,' Mandy said, as Puddles rolled over on the towel and began to lick listlessly at one wet paw.

'She needs a good sleep,' Mrs Hope said. Puddles was quickly drying off and her puppy fur had began to fluff out. It was streaked with very dark grey, almost black, and one of her feet was darker still.

'She's so tiny,' Jenny sighed. 'I love her one black sock.'

Mrs Hope gently slipped a syringe into Puddles' front leg. She hardly noticed the needle going in. Emily Hope taped a tiny tube into place, to carry saline solution into Puddles' body. The little puppy looked at her leg curiously, and tried to nibble at the tape.

'Come along, young lady,' said Mandy's mum lifting the sleepy puppy into her arms. Mandy picked up the plastic bottle that held the saline and followed her mother round the table and toward the door.

'I can see you've done this before! Jenny said quietly,

looking impressed. Mandy grinned, and nodded.

'I get plenty of practice here, she said.

In Animal Ark's residential unit, Mandy and her

mum put Puddles
into a small kennel
lined with a
fleecy rug. Mrs
Hope hung the
bag of saline on a
hook outside the
kennel and
carefully closed

the door. 'We must let her sleep. I'll check on her in a few hours' time,' Emily Hope said. 'Now, what about something to drink and a bite to eat for everyone?'

Mandy didn't feel very hungry. She wanted to stay and comfort the puppy. But Puddles' head had drooped on to her front paws and, as Mandy watched, she sighed deeply as her eyes closed.

'Right,' she said, smiling at her mum. 'That

sounds like a good idea.'

Six

The next
morning, Mandy
ran downstairs
and straight out

to the residential
unit to check on
their new patient.
   'She's had a
good long sleep,'
said Mr Hope.
'I've taken her
off the drip and,
my guess is, she's

ready for
something to eat.'
Mandy gazed in at
the little pup.
Puddles blinked
her blue eyes and
looked slowly
round her kennel,
as if trying to

remember where she was. Then she shuffled forward and put her wide, black, button nose up against the wire mesh, trying to sniff at Mandy.

'Can I take her out?' Mandy pleaded.

'I expect she'd like some attention.' Mr Hope grinned. He unlatched the kennel and stood aside. 'There you are. . . I'll go and find her some breakfast!'

Puddles sneezed violently as Mandy put her hands gently round her pink tummy. 'Oops! Bless you!' Mandy said, and lifted Puddles into her arms. The puppy's long fur was as soft as silk. She sniffed at Mandy's chin,

then found her
finger and began
to chew on it with
needle-sharp
teeth. 'Ouch!'
Mandy extracted
her finger. 'Here,
look what Dad's
got for you.'

Adam Hope had spooned some tinned chicken and rice into a bowl. It was a special mix for animals that had been ill. He held it under the puppy's nose. She whimpered and began to squirm in Mandy's arms to get free.

'All right,' Mandy laughed, putting her down. 'Now, don't

gobble it all at once or you might choke.'

Puddles ate daintily but hungrily, then licked the bowl clean with a small pink tongue. Then she sat down and licked her lips. Mandy laughed.

'How's she doing?' asked Emily Hope, appearing at the door of the residential unit.

'She's much better this morning, Mum,' Mandy told her happily. 'She's eaten and she seems more cheerful.' She looked at Puddles, who was taking small, hesitant steps around the floor. 'Can she go outside on the grass? She might want to....oh! Too late!'

'I'll see to it!'
Mrs Hope said.
'I'd offer to
help but I haven't
had my breakfast
yet!' Adam Hope
grinned. He
turned to Mandy.
'The puppy should

stay indoors a bit longer, Mandy. I want to be sure that she's free of infection. Oh, and by the way, I've written out a cheque for the money you collected yesterday, so you can post it later.'

'Thanks, Dad,' Mandy said. 'I want to make sure the money gets to the We Love Animals fund as

soon as possible.'
She waved to
Puddles who was
having her gums
examined by Mrs
Hope. 'I'll come
and see you
later,' she told
the puppy.

Adam Hope yawned. 'I'm starving. It's way past my breakfast time. Anyone for scrambled eggs?'

Mandy had just finished washing the last of the breakfast dishes when there was a knock on the kitchen door. It was James.

'Hi, Mandy.' He smiled as he flicked his fringe off his forehead. 'I came to see how that puppy is getting on.'

'Come in,' Mandy said,

moving aside to let him in. 'We checked on her this morning and she seems a bit better. But Dad says she has to stay in the kennel for a while.' She sat down on a kitchen chair opposite her friend. 'James, I've been thinking. . .' Mandy folded her arms.

'What about?'
James looked at
her warily. He
took off his
glasses and
polished them on
his sleeve.

'We ought to go
back to Mrs

Merrick's house,' Mandy said. 'I'm sure these poor puppies are something to do with her. We should see if we can find out anything.'

'How do you mean?' James asked, putting his glasses back on.

'I want to take a look around.' Mandy sounded fierce.

'Someone's got to do something.'

  'We'd have to be careful. Remember what Ted Forrester said. . .' James began.

'It'll be OK,'
Mandy said firmly.
'We can pretend. .
to be interested
in buying a puppy
and just ask some
questions.'

James was
doubtful. 'She

didn't want to talk to us last time.'

'But she thought we were collecting money. If we say we want to buy a puppy, she'll have to let

us in, won't she?'
Mandy reasoned.

'I suppose so,'
James said,
looking worried.
Then he
brightened. 'I
suppose we could
tell her about

finding Puddles, and see what her reaction is.'

'That's an idea.' Mandy threw the damp tea towel on to the rack. 'We'll go this morning.'

'OK,' James agreed. 'I'll go home and get my bike.'

'Will Jenny want to come with us?' Mandy asked. James shook his head. 'She's

waiting for a
phone call from
her parents.
They're travelling
around in Finland
on some sort of
coastguard
business and they
promised to ring

her this morning,' James explained, following Mandy out into the garden where Emily Hope was watering the roses.

'Hello, James,'
she smiled,
looking up from
her work.

'Hi, Mrs Hope,'
James replied.

'Mum,' Mandy
began, 'we're

going for a bike ride.'

'That sounds like a good idea. It's a lovely day,' Emily Hope said, looking up at the deep blue sky.

'We thought we'd go back over to Mrs Merrick's house and ask if we can see her puppies,' Mandy said casually.

'Well, I suppose there's no harm

in asking to see them.' Mrs Hope went back to her pruning. 'But, remember, she may not want you there. Just be careful and don't make a nuisance of yourself, will you?'

'We won't. Promise!' Mandy said. She turned eagerly to James. 'Meet you outside the post office in .ten minutes?'

'Right.' James waved as he headed off down the drive.

Mandy's heart was hammering slightly as she knocked on Mrs

Merrick's front door.

'Yes? Can I help you?' A girl of about seventeen stood in the doorway. She had a pale, oval face and thick chestnut-coloured hair that hung to her shoulders. Her fingers were looped through the collar of a large adult sheepdog.

'Yes, please,' Mandy smiled. 'Urn ... we would like to see the puppies.'

'My mother isn't here,' the girl told them. 'She's had to go

out. I'm Tracy.
Are you
interested in
buying a puppy?'
She frowned,
looked past
Mandy and James
as if expecting to

see their parents
in the driveway.
   'We know that
your mother
breeds Old
English
sheepdogs,'
Mandy explained.

'We'd love to see them...'

'If you've got any pups at the moment,' James put in, nudging Mandy with his elbow. Tracy suddenly smiled.

She rubbed her eyes and pushed the hair back off her face with her hands. She let go of the dog, who took a step forward and peered docilely up

at Mandy and
James through a
thick fringe of
white fur. Mandy
stroked its head.
She couldn't see
its eyes at all.

'Got any?
We've got twelve

at the moment,' Tracy told them. 'I'm exhausted looking after them all. You wouldn't believe what hard work they are.' Tracy stepped aside.

'Why don't you come in and take a look?'

'Oh, thank you so much!' Mandy said, relieved. They followed Tracy through the dim interior of the house, into a big kitchen with a tiled floor. A barricade of heavy crates had been used to confine the pups in the utility area. Mandy could hear faint whimpering and scuffling sounds, and a few louder, more determined howls. 'Over here,' Tracy was saying, sliding the heavy boxes to one side.

The puppies, seeing the strangers, shrank back, then scampered away to take refuge on a heap of old cushions in a large cardboard box.

The box had a large U-shape cut out of one side, so the puppies could hop in and out.

'Oh, look!' Mandy said, delighted with

the shaggy pups.
'Aren't they
gorgeous?'

Tracy said
nothing. She
folded her arms
across her chest.

'They're great!'
James exclaimed,

looking at the tangle of pale furry bodies and shining black noses. The puppies peeped out from behind each other and blinked at Mandy and James, but seemed reluctant to come near the strangers.

'Can we touch them?' Mandy asked Tracy. She nodded and yawned.

'Of course. I'm going to make myself a sandwich. I haven't had any breakfast yet and I'm starving. So if you wouldn't mind keeping an eye on them for me, that would be great,' she said. 'Don't let any escape, for heaven's sake!' She yawned again.

Mandy noticed shadows under Tracy's eyes. 'Oh,

don't worry.
We'll take care
of them. You have
a break,' Mandy
smiled.

A telephone
rang in the
hallway, and
Tracy sprinted

away to answer it.
The adult dog lay
down on the
kitchen floor and
Mandy and James
stepped over into
the puppies'
enclosure, pulling
the barricade

shut behind them.
One of the larger
pups gave a fierce
little growl and
took a step
forward, sniffing
at Mandy's
outstretched
fingers.

'Hello,' Mandy said softly, crouching down to greet the little dog. 'Come and say hello... Mandy expected the puppy to jump up at her. She loved

the comical
curiosity of
puppies, and the
way they
responded
trustingly to
anyone who was
kind to them. But
this pup was

different. He and
the other pups
seemed reluctant
to come near. The
puppy turned
round and
clambered back
into the box over
the heads of a

few smaller,
sleeping puppies.

'James!' Mandy
whispered. 'They
don't behave as
they should, do
they?'

'How do you
mean?' James

whispered back
He was kneeling
on the
newspapers and
had just noticed a
dark wet patch
spreading across
the fabric of his

jeans. He wrinkled his nose.

'Well, they don't seem playful or interested...' Mandy couldn't quite explain what was wrong.

'Probably sleepy,' James said. 'Shh, that girl's coming back.'

Tracy came into the kitchen, her sandals making a little tapping

sound on the tiles.
She buttered a
slice of bread and
then hunted
about in the
fridge for
something.

Mandy stood up.
'The pups are all

so sweet,' she said to Tracy. 'How on earth do people choose?'

'Do you want a male or female? That's a start,' Tracy said without turning round. She was slicing cheese from a big yellow block. Mandy looked at James, who shrugged at her. 'Um ... a girl, probably,' Mandy said quickly.

James had
started creeping
across the
expanse of
newspaper with
his fingers
stretched out,
trying to coax a
tiny puppy

forwards. It whimpered, then yawned and toppled over. The adult dog wandered over to the barricade and put its large, square muzzle

over the top to
look in.

'What an
enormous litter!'
Mandy said,
wondering why
the puppies
varied in size
quite as much as

they did. Tracy glanced over her shoulder. 'We've got a mixed bunch here - about four separate litters,' she said, through a mouthful of cheese sandwich.

'Maybe more -
I've lost count.'
   'What?' Mandy
asked. 'Really?
How come?' She
stood up,
frowning.
   'Well, my
mother does run a

business here, you know,' Tracy said sharply. Mandy decided it was best not to ask any more questions. Tracy yawned again and rubbed her eyes.

'Here, Troy. Here, boy!' Tracy called the adult dog to her side.

'Can we help you with the puppies, Tracy?' Mandy asked hopefully. 'I mean, James and I love dogs. We'd love to spend some time helping to feed them, or clean up or something anything.'

'Yes, we really would,' James

confirmed. He had pulled a puppy into his lap and was fiddling with its tiny ears.

'Really?' Tracy had brightened. She came over, her sandwich in her hand. 'I could really use some help. They're due for a clean out, as you can probably smell. And feeding them all is a nightmare - some of the little ones are still on bottles.' Then she hesitated. 'I can't pay you, you know.'

'Oh, we don't want any money!' Mandy told her. Then, she asked the question she had been trying to hold back. 'Where is ... where are ... the mother dogs?'

'Look, I told you,' Tracy said, 'we're running a

business here. I've had to give up college to help my mother, you know and...'

To Mandy's horror, she saw that Tracy's eyes

were wet with tears.

'Right,' said James, getting quickly to his feet. 'Where do you keep the bucket and mop?' he asked. 'Let's make a start.'

'Oh, look, I'm sorry,' Tracy said miserably. 'It's just that I'm tired, really. I didn't mean to snap at you.'

'That's all right,' Mandy smiled. 'We'd like to help. What can we do?'

'You know, we found an Old English sheepdog puppy just like

these,' James said suddenly. 'It was wandering outside the Fox and *Goose* in Welford.'

Tracy, who was delving into a tall cupboard in

search of a
bucket, spun
round and stared
at James.
'Really?' she
asked, her eyes
wide.
   'Yes,' Mandy
said in what she

hoped was a casual voice. 'It's very young and it was in a terrible state. My mum and dad are vets, and they've been looking after it in the residential unit at Animal Ark.'

'What did it look like?' Tracy asked anxiously.

James looked at Mandy. 'About twelve or thirteen weeks,

we think,' Mandy
told her. 'But it
was very thin and
sad-looking - and
its coat was in a
terrible mess,'
Mandy finished.
  'One very dark
grey foot - the

other three
white?' Tracy
asked, her voice
hopeful.

'Yes, that's it.
Exactly,' Mandy
confirmed.

'Petal!' Tracy
breathed,

covering her face with her hands. 'Petal! I can't believe it! You found her! Is she safe? Is she all right?'

'She is one of your puppies!'

Mandy cried.
'She's fine,
Tracy,' she added
reassuringly.
'Don't worry.
She's dehydrated
because she's had
a tummy upset, so
she's a bit weak

but. . .' Mandy
stopped. Tracy's
thin shoulders
were heaving.
From behind the
hands that
covered her face
Mandy and James

could hear
muffled sobs.

Seven

Tracy Merrick
was crying noisily.
Mandy looked at
James in alarm

and he shrugged his shoulders. She stepped across the barricade of crates and hurried to Tracy's side. 'Don't cry, Tracy,' she pleaded. 'Puddles - Petal - is safe. What happened to her?'

Tracy sniffed loudly. 'Mum was furious,' she mumbled through her tears. 'It was quite a few days ago, now. I must have left the barricade open and Petal squeezed through. She was the liveliest of the litter. She was always trying to escape and explore. She got out of the kitchen door and I didn't notice. Then, when I went to open the front door...'

James put the sheepdog puppy he'd been playing with back on the cushion and joined Mandy and Tracy. Troy, the adult dog, was staring mournfully up at Tracy.

'Well, it's good news that she's safe, isn't it?' Mandy asked, wishing Tracy would stop crying. Her nose had

gone very red and
her skin was
blotchy.

'I suppose so,'
Tracy said,
sniffing. 'It's
just that - well,
we've got too
many puppies and

when mum has to go out... I thought...' she paused and gasped, covering her face again, 'I thought that Petal was dead!

She was my favourite, too.'

'It's OK, Tracy,' Mandy said, soothingly. 'We found her and she's doing fine. You could come and visit her

at Animal Ark.'
Mandy didn't
want Tracy to
take Puddles back.
Mrs Merrick
would only sell
the puppy. Tracy
had said herself
that the puppies

were only a business.

Tracy snatched a tissue from a box on a small kitchen table, then. . sat down with a heavy sigh. She blew her nose loudly, making Troy prick up his ears.

'Yes,' she said wearily. 'I'd like to come and see Petal - as soon as I can get away. Now...' Suddenly

Tracy sat up straight and businesslike. 'I need to get to work. Mum will be so relieved if everything's done when she gets home.'

'Has she been away for long?' Mandy asked, eyeing the pile of unwashed dishes and the general mess in the kitchen.

'She went out early this morning. She's having problems with the bank,' Tracy confided hesitantly. 'Her bank manager wanted to meet her today to try and sort things out.'

'Shall I fill a bucket and wash this floor?' James suggested helpfully.

'Yes, please. There's one in that cupboard,' Tracy said, pointing. She had stopped crying, Mandy saw with relief. 'Mandy,' she asked, 'would you collect the dirty newspaper and throw it in that bin-bag for me? I'll go and start making up the milk formula.'

When Tracy had gone out of the

kitchen, Mandy turned to James. 'No mother dogs!' she hissed. 'That's awful. People are coming here and buying these puppies without having seen them with their mother.'

'Where do you think she's getting all the puppies from, then, if there are no mother dogs here?' James sounded puzzled.

'I don't know,' Mandy told him, frowning. 'But I know my mum and dad wouldn't like it. You're supposed to see

pups with their
mother when you
buy one.'

Mandy stepped
gently over the
barricade and
three plump little
puppies shuffled
out of her way. In

the box, some of
the pups were
still asleep,
snuggled up
tightly together
with their legs
intertwined, so
that it was
difficult to tell

where one pup
ended and
another began.
Mandy longed to
pick them up and
play with them
but, somehow,
these puppies
didn't seem very

interested in playing.

'She's really upset, isn't she? Tracy, I mean,' James observed, dipping his mop into a bucket. 'We'd better not

ask her anymore
questions. She
might get upset
again.'

'Hmm,' said
Mandy, torn
between her
anger about the
motherless

puppies and her
sympathy for
Tracy. 'She said
she had to give up
college to help
her mum out,' she
remembered. 'I
wonder what
happened so that

her mum couldn't
cope?'

'It does sound
strange,' James
agreed. Mandy
had heaped the
soiled newspapers
into a pile,
clearing an area

of floor space for James's mop. The puppies had retreated into the big cardboard box and sat staring out with nervous expressions on their tiny faces.

'Oh, look at them, James!' Mandy sighed, getting down on her knees to look. 'Aren't they great?' An assortment of blue and black eyes looked back solemnly at her. 'I wish I could have one,' she confessed.

The kitchen door squeaked as

Tracy came back in carrying two large tins of a puppy milk formula. 'This is Tina,' she announced, as she put the tins down on the worktop.

'She's been snoozing in the sun, haven't you, darling?' Mandy looked up at a very large Old English sheepdog standing at Tracy's side. She had a bright orange beard of hair round her muzzle and her shaggy coat was a pale grey-blue in colour.

'Oh! Hello!' Mandy said to the

dog, which towered over her as she kneeled on the floor.

'She's my mum's special dog,' Tracy said. 'She's had quite a few litters in her time. She's a wonderful mum.'

James rested the mop in the bucket and went forward with Mandy to pet Tina.'

Tracy began measuring the

milk powder into a bowl. 'Tina and Troy were show dogs. My mother doesn't show any longer, so they have a quieter life now, really.' Tracy poured warm water from a kettle into a measuring jug.

'They must need a lot of grooming,' James said, running his fingers through Tina's thick coat.

'We comb them out about once a week,' Tracy said, pouring the water on to the milk powder. 'They need regular grooming, or their coats can get very tangled and matted.'

James started mopping the floor. The puppies scampered away into their box, and peeped nervously out from the hole. Mandy watched Tracy making up milk for three bottles. 'These feeding bottles are used for premature babies,' Tracy told her, as she whisked the milk into a froth.

'Doesn't Tina feed any of the puppies herself?' Mandy asked, puzzled.

'None of these are Tina's pups,' Tracy explained. 'The last of her litter had been sold when these came to us. They're all Old English pups but

different ages
and from
different litters.'
  Mandy tried not
to look horrified.
'Can I feed one
of them?' she
asked.

'I'll help!'
James called.
'I've finished
doing the floor.'
  'All right,'
Tracy agreed.
She screwed the
tops on to the
bottles and

handed one to Mandy. It was warm. 'You get started with these. They're for the three very small, dark-coloured pups asleep in the box.

I'll make up the food for the older ones.' She smiled suddenly. 'Thanks for helping,' she. said. 'We love helping animals, don't we,

James?' Mandy said.

James nodded and held out an eager hand for the bottle.

Mandy sat cross-legged on the floor in the

clean enclosure, with James beside her. She lifted a puppy on to her lap. It whimpered in protest at having been disturbed from a warm and cosy sleep. Mandy stroked the pup's wrinkled little brow and held the rubbery teat of the bottle to its mouth. The puppy's nose twitched, then, with its eyes still closed, it grabbed on to the teat and began sucking hard. James reached into the big box and gently lifted another puppy.

'Wow,' said
James, surprised
at the little dog's
strength as it

began to suck.
'How old are
these puppies,
Tracy?'
   'Not sure. . .'
Tracy replied
vaguely. 'Those
are about four or
five weeks, I

think. Some are older.' James looked across at Mandy, who was frowning angrily. She knew that puppies weren't supposed to leave their mother until they were at least six weeks old. Surely any breeder ought to know that too.

'They're so cute,' James said quickly. 'Mine's a girl. What's yours,

Mandy?' Mandy looked down at the puppy in her lap. It was lying on its back, and pedalling in the air with its front paws, concentrating on drinking up the warm milk as fast as possible. 'Um, let's see ... it's a boy!' she said.

Tracy was carrying over a series of shallow dishes brimming

with minced meat
and puppy meal.
'The bigger pups
are on four meals
a day,' she told
them with a small
shake of her head.
'Feeding and
clearing up, then

feeding again... it never ends.'

The puppy in Mandy's lap had finished his bottle and was sitting on the floor, licking his lips. He looked up

at Mandy with
sad dark eyes.
She stroked him
softly, murmuring,
'Good boy.' The
puppy took a
wobbly step
towards her and
climbed, over her

legs, curling up in the warmth and safety of her lap. He belched softly, then sighed and blinked up at Mandy. Mandy ruffled the silky little head and breathed in the smell of puppy and warm, sweet milk.

'You are a little sweetie,' she whispered. The puppy closed his eyes. Mandy wondered where his mother was.

She looked up at Tracy. 'Did the mothers of all of these puppies die?' she asked sadly.

Tracy was laying out the puppies' dishes on the floor of the enclosure. As the puppies tumbled forward, eager for food, she separated them into groups of three and encouraged them by pressing on their noses.

'I don't know,' Tracy replied absently. 'We've never seen the mothers. They came to us to be sold on. My mother agreed to take on one litter, as a favour, and we've had nothing but trouble since!'

'Trouble?'
Mandy asked,
taking the second
bottle of milk
Tracy offered
her. 'What kind
of trouble?'

James was
frowning at

Mandy. 'My puppy has gone to sleep!' he announced, trying to change the subject. 'Do you want to feed the third one, Mandy?' But

Mandy only nodded.

'We've been overwhelmed by puppies needing homes,' Tracy confessed, tucking her springy hair behind her ears. 'Mum's having to sell them at less than half the proper price, and it's costing us a fortune to take care of them all.' She sighed crossly and plucked a greedy puppy out of its dish. Then she groaned as it began to trample a gooey mess of meat and meal across the floor.

'I really want to get back to college - but I can't,' Tracy went on. 'Mum can't cope on her own - not with all this lot!'

Mandy thought Tracy was going to cry again, so she said quickly, 'Well, that's those two full of milk. Any more?'

'No more.'

Tracy shook her

head. 'But, we'll need to put down fresh newspaper in a hurry or they'll begin to make a mess on the floor.' James leaped to his feet. 'Right!' he said.

'I'll get some. Where do you keep it?'

'Bottom of the broom cupboard,' Tracy told him. 'Thanks.'

'I can fluff up the cushions in

the box,' Mandy
suggested.

'If you like.'
Tracy smiled.
Mandy waited
while James
spread
newspapers on
the floor, then,

very gently, she lifted each of the puppies in turn out of the box. They huddled together on the floor, looking bewildered. Mandy untied the lace on one of her trainers and danced it about in front of the pups. One crept forward to investigate but Mandy couldn't

persuade him to
have a game.

Eventually
Mandy gave up.
She shook out the
large cushion in
the box, and
plumped up the
smaller ones.

Then she put the younger puppies back into their bed. They snuggled together, making little mewling sounds.

James sighed as he spotted a

fresh puddle spreading across the clean newspapers. 'Phew! I see what you mean. It is hard work.' He looked at his watch. 'Mandy,

we ought to go
home now.'

'Yes.' Mandy
stroked each of
the pups in turn.
'We'd better.'
She glanced at
Tracy, who
seemed cheerful

enough now. She was eating an apple and smiling.

'So which puppy do you want to buy?' she asked. Mandy looked at James in horror, trying to

remember exactly
what she had said
to Tracy earlier
that morning.

'Um. . . how
much are they?'
James said.
'£200 each,'
Tracy said, 'but

my mum might give you a discount.'

'Oh, that's far more than we could afford to spend,' Mandy said, quickly. 'I'm sorry. I hadn't realised they would be quite so expensive.'

'Pure breeds are always expensive,' Tracy pointed out.

'We'll have to save up,' James

shrugged.
'Thanks for letting us play with them.'

'Thanks for your help. I wish you could come every day,' Tracy sighed.

'We could come again,' Mandy offered at once. 'It's school holidays now. We've got plenty of time. Can we come again?'

'Of course!'
Tracy laughed.
'If you don't
mind working!
Come on, I'll show
you out.'